Dear Clueless,

By York Liverpool

ISBN: 0984682910
ISBN-13: 978-0-9846829-1-1

Library of Congress Control Number: 2011939936
Yorkpool Publishing, Montgomery Village, MD

This book is entirely a work of fiction. Names, characters, events, and the company are as a result of the author's imagination. Any similarities to people, alive or dead, activities or events, are completely coincidental.

Dedication

In loving memory of my mother, Merlene Elaine, a woman who exemplified true perseverance, encouraged my curiosity, and instilled in me an insatiable love for learning.

Acknowledgements

This book would not have been possible without the support and encouragement of many people. I would like to thank my siblings, Carolyn, Orville, Jr., Cheryl, Andrew, and Michael, as well as my brother-in-law, Rohan, for believing in me. Also, Richelle Charles, Maria Moreno, and Raphael Todd, for conveying genuine enthusiasm as content and characters developed. Last, but not least, I would like to acknowledge Chief for demonstrating the importance of becoming and being one's authentic self regardless of the cost.

Preface

Dear Reader,

Learning how to successfully negotiate organizational politics is no easy feat. Many people are befuddled by the daily ambiguous and unforgiving social transactions that have nothing to do with achieving their organization's mission and everything to do with power plays among impoverished personalities.

Much to the dismay of some and the delight of others, organizational politics is a game where the rules are senseless, and inhumanity is indefinitely perpetuated. Countless employees either find themselves incapable of learning the bizarre social politics of their company, or become so entrenched in them that they lose themselves. Some simply give notice because they would rather join an unemployment line than continue to drink an inebriating and numbing cocktail of "pamper egos, kowtow, shamelessly agree, and turn a blind eye."

Interestingly, there are quite a few people who knowingly and unknowingly forge relationships, particularly mentoring relationships, to help them better navigate political landmines and secure the rewards that learning how to *advantageously* manage organizational politics might yield. Clueless, a seemingly naïve protégé of a powerful and well-positioned businessman, found himself in such a relationship.

Clueless' mentor's approach to sorting him out might be offensive and, appear unnecessarily harsh and absent of civility. But, mentoring relationships are as different as the mentors and mentees themselves. Undoubtedly, there are some ruthless mentors who school their mentees in the ways of impiety. Yet, there are those, however few, who engage in mentoring to impart good things and worthwhile lessons—the better and best part of who they have become. Whether for good or for ill, any mentor's ultimate goal is to provide perspective and guide the mentee to a proper and practical understanding of complex organizational politics.

Sincerely,
York Liverpool

Letter 1

Dear Clueless,

I found your letter to be quite exasperating and disquieting. In the future, do not trouble me with lengthy, outlandish rationalizations on the Peter Principle and its possible relevance today. The untried opinion that a person is promoted to his or her level of incompetence is immaterial. What should be praised is that, given the circumstances, s/he arose at all.

Is your glass always half-empty on professional, personal, and political matters? Well, permit me to fill it with bitter truth. Work is simply an extension of high school. The characters are the same, but the roles are intensified by money, position, and power. My only advice to you in this regard is that when you choose your character, choose wisely. I would rather you be a triumphant scoundrel veiled behind the plastic smile and false eyelashes of a prom queen, than a disregarded, bullied hall monitor adorned in ill-fitted clothing.

To help you along your troubled professional path, I offer you another timeless piece of advice—find ambition. She is probably hiding in plain sight, perhaps in your neighbor's ornately decorated backyard. Woo her. Or, perhaps she sits quietly yet eagerly in the back-seat of one of his five leased luxury cars. Locate and commandeer her.

Once you do, remember that ambition is a funny mistress. Master her, and the possibilities are endless. Permit her to master you, and your greatest nightmares will haunt you beyond the grave.

Understand this, if you cannot successfully negotiate this small hurdle, you are no mentee of mine. And for goodness' sake, stay away from those bloody self-help books. You did not graduate from the number-one business school in the country to later grow a conscience. Leave matters of conscience to hall monitors, and the like.

Affectionately,

A. Scélérat

Albert Scélérat
Chief Global Strategist
Global Spectrum Alliance Inc.

Letter 2

Dear Clueless,

I was astonished to read in your letter that you had been promoted to Interim Assistant Director of Domestic Affairs after the untimely death of the former occupant. Mark my words, if he had not succumbed to whatever beckoned him beyond this life, you would have labored and languished for at least five cruel years beneath his heels.

People of his sort are as complacent as they are dim-witted. They allow sentiment and anecdotes of retiring in some nondescript, overpriced beach house to compel them to adorn, and without fail, flaunt professional pretense for forty measly hours every week. I despise the lot of them. Talentless and devoid of the true unbridled passion of an executive mercenary.

It is my understanding that he was very much like his predecessor—average and naïve. He too permitted the corner office, with its grand windows, to lull him into a deep sleep and strangle his aspirations. People like them reflect so poorly on those of us who scrupulously master the fine art of organizational politics. Only an act of God can remove such insufferable deadwoods from their makeshift perches.

Dear Clueless

I hope that your "time of mourning" for this man, as you so expressively described it, was resourcefully earnest, yet brief. When it comes to the death of a colleague, you do not want to be judged by others to be disingenuous; nevertheless, you also do not want to demonstrate an uncustomary, prolonged sense of emotional vulnerability for every warm body that makes a swift departure. I strongly admonish you to seize this opportunity (a clearly undeserved, but timely gift) to secure additional territory in the hearts and minds of your superiors.

From this new strategic vantage point, you must methodically shape their impressions of you. Manipulate their thinking by creating an illusion of who you aspire to be, but are not. Make them yearn for you like a man yearns for his young mistress upon witnessing his wife's worn body yawn chaotically under faint moonlight. Craft an image of yourself with such tactical precision that even when you think of it, regardless of its intricate falsities, it strikes fear and reverence in your own heart.

Whatever you do, do not make that corner office your home. Leave it sparsely decorated and permit its undressed walls to drive out the slightest suggestion of idleness and stupidity. I assure you that by doing so you will not only avoid the path of complacency, but also an untimely death. Warmest regards,untimely death.

Warmest regards,

A. Scélérat

Albert Scélérat
Chief Global Strategist
Global Spectrum Alliance Inc.

Letter 3

Dear Clueless,

I received your delayed correspondence. I would not have opened it if I had known that it would be littered with misgivings and bitter complaints. You disappoint me. It has only been eight months. Are the office windows not grand enough for you? Is the vintage leather chair an ill fit? The color green suits you. Did you not know that terms like *interim* and *acting* are synonyms for *puppet* and *placeholder?* Must I instruct you in everything? Bathe you, dress you, feed you, wipe your ass, and demonstrate how to profitably sow seed? I knew your promotion was premature, yet still needful. After all, I do have a reputation to protect and an image to uphold.

Now, in regard to your unsophisticated discourse on job satisfaction, permit me to educate you. Job satisfaction is a product of your ability, or lack thereof, to master the arts of self promotion, ingratiation, and manipulation. These three factors are critical to the success of your quest to comprehensively serve your self-interests at every level of the company. Always remember, the greater good is your good and yours alone.

To produce job satisfaction, the only people you must *esteem* (albeit briefly and insincerely) more highly than yourself are those in and outside of the organization who possess a tactical advantage superior to yours. These individuals are both friend and foe. Keep them all close. Everyone else is dispensable—including your new charge.

According to my sources, you seem to be quite enamored with your administrative aid. Is it the soft curve of her hips or the venom in her floral perfume that has rendered you witless? There is no shame in the appreciation of eye candy. In my prime, I tasted more than my share, and even in the twilight of my years, with some prescribed assistance, I still occasionally indulge. However, at this stage in the game when lust parades so brazenly before you as she does, it can only serve as a superfluous distraction. For now, view the novelty in her beauty and the firmness of her breasts as liabilities. You do not want to be accused, falsely or otherwise, of lecherous behavior. Rid yourself of her. Do not promote, but supplant her. Recommendations for the location of her lateral transfer, and a more suitable, racially ambiguous and competent replacement are enclosed. Once you have created vast and unquestionable distance between you and this commoner, bed her if you must, but do not breed her. In due time (and for the sake of my reputation, probably quickly), *we* will find you a trophy whose beauty rivals Cleopatra's and status extends beyond Jackie Onassis. Until then, make your rounds; network and pilfer a grand and viable idea or two from an underling. As it stands, your contributions to the company are unremarkable and sorely lacking.

If you heed my counsel, you will not only scale unimaginable heights, but also erect new ones. The job satisfaction that you so absurdly crave is found in self-service. In the future, save your moaning and groaning for activities more appropriately suited.

Fondly,

Albert Scélérat
Chief Global Strategist
Global Spectrum Alliance Inc.

Letter 4

Dear Clueless,

The *talks*, as you so aptly christened them, to drop the *Interim* before Assistant Director of Domestic Affairs are not only authentic, but have been carefully orchestrated by me and will be executed by HR by the end of the month. Initially, some self-righteous prick wanted to announce the position and create a pool of internal and external applicants. To avert this catastrophe, I immediately exposed the fiscal recklessness in his procedurally correct idea. In truth, if the company posted the position, I would have been hard-pressed to convince members of the search committee to select you over a more worthy and qualified applicant. Learn this lesson now, and learn it well: most times doing what is right, is not doing what is right. It matters very little now. Your current position at the company is now secure. However, I wish I could say that was true of your future ascent.

As of last week, shifts in the economic and political landscape have changed how we do business. Our expansion into Asia means new blood—talented and eager blood—has flooded our organization's waters. Consequently, I need an additional pair of eyes and ears mulling about the American division of the company.

While I hoped for more practiced ones, yours will have to do—for now.

Your maiden voyage begins at your first high-level meeting next Monday. You will turn every trick I have taught you and acquire new ones. I have enclosed a comprehensive list of key players with their corresponding idiosyncrasies, proclivities, and fragile pacts. Study it. Study them. Make sure that you are the first to arrive and the last to leave. Drink very little before and during the meeting. Moreover, never exit the room to relieve yourself. Wear a diaper if you must, but your mind and body must be present at all times for all things.

During this meeting, and all meetings thereafter, observe and listen to everything. If someone doodles, sneezes, coughs, scratches an itch, stutters, belches impolitely, shifts in his or her seat, nurses a drink, gazes out a window, at a wall or table, gives his or her neighbor a quick glance, raises a brow, rolls an eye, nervously taps a pen, or suffers a stroke, take careful note of it. Conflicts of interest, alliances made, unmade, or fortified, and decisions pending or written in stone take many forms. Groupthink will prevail like an alpha male mounting a bitch in heat. Publicly, remain neutral in your discourse (a list of do's and don'ts are also enclosed), but privately seduce all. Cater to the distortions latent in their egos and the unpredictability of their insecurities. Like you, they all want and need something. Your job is to consistently and accurately ascertain what and how you can give them some of what they want and little of what they need. In the long run, this will serve you and me.

From now on, you will see evil, hear evil, speak evil, and know evil. Occasionally, you will be the instrument of...well, evil. In time your conscience will become seared. Until then, secure a priest or a shrink.

The politically charged and polarized waters of our company are tumultuous and unforgiving, yet they yield rewards to those who can bravely ride each tide. To be forewarned is to be forearmed. Assistant Director of Domestic Affairs, use the recently acquired surety of your title to gain an advantage. Do not embarrass me.

Yours truly,

Albert Scélérat
Chief Global Strategist
Global Spectrum Alliance Inc.

Letter 5

Dear Clueless,

I must admit that upon returning from Tokyo, the content of your letter was a source of wild amusement. I had no idea that you possessed such bottomless guile. There is hope for you yet.

It is true. Most women are catty and revengeful. You must continue to exploit this invaluable knowledge of the weaker sex. Their power not only lies in their tears and the warmth between their legs, but in their ability to hold and systematically act on grudges. They are the most unforgiving creatures, and they behave in subtle and unseemly ways to poison the well. This bane in their gender transcends color, culture, and coin.

Women are the reason politically charged work environments are spawned and endure. Women, through folly, fabrication, fickleness, and faithlessness, fuel the flames of discord and favoritism. Little do they know, pray for our sake that they do remain ignorant of this, they also possess the power to change it. The tongue is a small, but potent weapon indeed.

By nature, women are industrious. To their credit, they are wise healers and unfailing nurturers. When courage and the facility to lead are married to the innate distinctiveness of their species, their impact and contributions are unrivaled. Companies and countries in turmoil, or poised for a specific type of change, are more likely to place a woman at the helm than a man. Or, they install a capable man connected to a powerful female personality. It is a deeply held secret and most difficult to discover or puzzle out.

You must keep the women in your unit and beyond distracted, pacified, and indebted to you. Encourage the cattiness among them. This will keep them from forging alliances and supporting one another. Do small favors for them. Discover what each of them values and create currency. If they have children, or are a caregiver for a parent, periodically grant them additional time off. If they like a challenge, have them create and manage special projects. But remember, only attach your name to the projects that are successful. We cannot afford for you to be associated with failure. Furthermore, if any of your concubines hint at not receiving appropriate credit for their contributions, deflect. Like a good shepherd, guide them into a false sense of security through the use of praise and assurances. Use the *employee of the month* gimmick. If these women persist, remind them that any and everything they do is for the greater good of the company. Convince them that as a result of your unconditional support and encouragement, they were able to successfully execute their ideas—ones that you would have thought of anyway. Make them believe it. Make yourself believe it.

Women tend to carelessly misplace their need to be liked, equal, in control, validated, and affirmed. Everything is or becomes personal to and for them. Consequently, it causes them to reinforce the status quo like wicked pyromancers casting endless spells. Use this to your advantage, and quickly seize every opportunity to manipulate their weakness. Within reason, allow them to unburden themselves of both professional and private matters, but make sure trust goes unreciprocated. Only share information that is inconsequential. Nurture them, and inevitably they will yield their fruit, ripe and unripe.

When you least expect it, you will be promoted—to what, I know not. Let's just hope that your future elevation will not be as a result of the death of another colleague.

Congratulations on your engagement. I look forward to witnessing the lavish joining of two lives and the unavoidable clashing of two histories. As you are aware, Amina is her parents' only living child. Thus, in matters of business and finance, her father groomed her like the son he lost, and her mother raised her like a woman who only needs a man for one thing. Tread carefully, or risk castration, or something far worse—impoverishment.

Best regards,

Albert Scélérat
Chief Global Strategist
Global Spectrum Alliance Inc.

Letter 6

Dear Clueless,

I now understand that I cannot mince words with you. How you can be remarkably lucid regarding the foolhardiness of women and so utterly confused about everything else escapes me. In your letter you wrote, *"I attended the professional development series, "Discovering and Developing Your Leadership Style"…aspects of facilitative leadership are attractive and can be readily applied in my division."* After briefly turning your statement over in my head, the ensuing migraine spoke to me and said, "You have overestimated his ability to reason."

Are you bound eternally to ignorance? Professional development is the quintessential alternate reality—to put it mildly, an organizational occult. It is a place where employees are transformed into lab rats and fed some ill-conceived concoction of fiction and fantasy. The classes and content are an ingenious charade. We have hired imbeciles to teach foolishness. Leaders and managers alike disparage the content and govern as they please.

Ironically, everyone knows that professional development is a blatant waste of company time and money. However, no one will address the matter because it serves a sinister, yet meaningful, purpose: the perpetuation of ignorance and sweeping pacification. Continue to periodically attend and involve yourself in the occultist activities. It will augment your marketability and make you look better in the eyes of those above you. Nonetheless, while your attendance is advantageous, please try to recall that everything taught is pure, unadulterated, useless rubbish.

As for your facilitative leadership, your attraction is misplaced and should be directed toward efforts to breed your wife. Facilitative leadership is theoretical pretense masquerading as employee empowerment. Using it will only engender false hope and anxiety in subordinates. It will also generate a cesspool of insubordination and insurrection among the weak and mindless. If you value your future at this company, avoid using "*aspects of facilitative leadership*" like a new inmate avoids dropping a bar of soap during the morning shower.

I hope you are faring far better in your marriage than you are at work. Or do you need concepts of facilitative leadership to assist you to perform your marital duties? It has been four months since the day of your circus-laden nuptials and still no word regarding the creation of offspring to solidify your financial future. Know your priorities.

Best Always,

A. Scélérat

Albert Scélérat
Chief Global Strategist
Global Spectrum Alliance Inc.

Letter 7

Dear Clueless,

You must vanquish these childish notions that are pervasive throughout your letters. There is a comprehensible difference between appearance and reality. Your supervisor appears to like you. But truth be told, he would rather you walk blindfolded into oncoming traffic. Your wife's family appears to tolerate you, but the reality is your insatiable lust to be pleasured has produced their first grandchild, and therefore, through blood, they are now irrevocably beholden to you. Appearances take on a romantic allure that is only remedied by the bitter taste of reality. As you know firsthand, even pleasure carries a vile, yet intoxicating, stench.

You remind me of a woman plagued by morning sickness, but who labors under the romanticized delusion of the joys of pregnancy and childbirth as her hips swell to unsightly proportions and she retches in her kitchen sink. I am puzzled by your profound state of childlike bewilderment. Your match with Amina was made solely to improve your status, not to make you happy.

Allow me to put your troubled mind at ease—you are inconsequential. Amina is her parents' sun, moon, and stars. Their grandson is the blood that courses decisively through their veins. Your contribution, or rather *role*, as husband is symbolic at best. Do not put too much emotional or mental stock in marriage and family, or you will suffer the fate of your less-talented peers and become one the biggest casualties of familial fraud.

Create another galaxy or two in Amina's womb. I am almost positive that her mother would be most grateful for another female to twist into her image. If your soldiers are up to the task, twin girls would probably throw your mother-in-law into a shopping frenzy and establish the basis for certain clauses in your prenuptial agreement to be renegotiated.

As difficult as I know this is for you, do try to remain rational even when aspects of marriage and family, and the *feelings* they seem to produce so strongly in you, refuse to yield to rationality. Do not allow these relationships to distract you. Like me, you can always remarry and have more children. Or, if it pleases you, join the ranks of Larry King and Elizabeth Taylor.

Continue to keep up with appearances, but stay firmly grounded in this reality: Amina and her son are the unfailing dawn, steadfast dusk, and all things in between. You are the sperm donor. Only what you can produce to benefit others truly matters. Once your currency deteriorates, you will be put out to pasture and unceremoniously shot.

Clueless, your career is what you make your own. It is a life experience that you can carefully weave into something magnificent and legendary. Raise the level of your value.

More later,

Albert Scélérat
Chief Global Strategist
Global Spectrum Alliance Inc.

Letter 8

Dear Clueless,

I am quite relieved that you have recovered from your bout of temporary insanity. As you now know, family life can be dreadfully taxing and unrewarding. It is laden with ambiguity. Spouses are far too demanding and struggle needlessly for a level of respect and control in the relationship that is not due them. Instead of marrying, it would have been infinitely wiser if you had purchased a litter of Labrador retrievers or boxers. At least you could have bred and sold them without consequence or too much remorse. I will instruct you on how to strategically divest yourself of Amina and her growing brood at a later date.

Lesson number 1,137: You must learn to properly sort out what is important from what is trivial. So what, your supervisor used you as a scapegoat and then ripped you a new one. Did you expect differently? My six-year-old granddaughter and her dog, Paprika, could have easily accomplished the same feat. So what if he used the company's employee evaluation system to make you look like an incompetent, drooling mongrel in need of training and retraining. Is there any truth to it? If my memory serves me correctly—and it does—you were newly sworn in as a eunuch in the temple of professional development. To better negotiate this trifling incident, why don't you ask the high priestess of training to return your shaft and your balls so that you can have them surgically reattached?

You should know by now that your supervisor is a clever bastard—both figuratively and literally. What he lacks in pedigree, he has made up for in ability and stealth. You are excessively trusting. He merely sees and creates opportunities to capitalize on this flaw in your character, which, unbeknownst to me for some bloody reason, you refuse to actively manage. What do you expect a shark to do when it smells and tastes blood in the water? You do not labor in a world of right and wrong—just wrong and very wrong.

I strongly suggest that you do not conduct yourself like a prattling, ill-tempered woman. Return the favor. But whatever you do (a list of suggestions are enclosed), do it in such a way that ensures he would rather soil himself in public than inconvenience you, and consequently me, ever again.

As for his methods, they are amateurish. The noose that I would have set about your neck would have strangled you for ten life-times before I relaxed it. You would know that I was screwing you and enjoying every waking minute of it. While you were off somewhere frolicking on some beach with your wife and 1.4 children, I would have spun a web that would have had you reassigned to a small village in Siberia without a salary increase, indoor plumbing, or heat.

In regard to the *issue* you wrote about. The answer is quite simple. Always side with the employee that you can manipulate the most or like the best. Disregard the facts and your feelings. Merely make assumptions and act decisively on those assumptions. Your primary objective should always be to protect your interests.

Regards,

Albert Scélérat
Chief Global Strategist
Global Spectrum Alliance Inc.

Letter 9

Dear Clueless,

I am uncertain if I understand the reasoning behind the question you posed in your sixty-fourth...or was it your sixty-fifth letter? My apologies. I am afraid that due to the frequency and length of your discourse, I have lost count and, occasionally, interest. Be that as it may, I found this particular letter and your question, *"What if a person is constitutionally incapable of deception?"* most intriguing. It is now becoming clear to me that your artless simplicity is only surpassed by your ignorance.

The fact that you think it possible for someone to be incapable of deception is a strong indication that you continue to labor under idealistic delusions that negatively impact your evaluation of reality. Deception, whether you are on the giving or receiving end of it, is the foundation of civilizations past and present. Before the first woman spread her legs to begin your bloodline, great nations were built and savaged, fortunes made and unmade, all in the indecipherable grasp of deception. Some people are simply more practiced at it than others.

Evidently, your head continues to float aimlessly in the clouds that hover about your windows. How is it that

27

you fail to notice that everyone, including the pretentious brat that sucks greedily at your wife's swollen breast, is practicing deception?

Since your *constitution* is so damnably delicate, think of practicing deception like making and sharing a cake—a chocolate cake. Throughout the years I have noticed that whether people like chocolate or not, they compel themselves to indulge to not look like the odd man out. But I digress. Like the making of a chocolate cake, deception requires certain essential ingredients. The combination of the following thirteen components is necessary to bake a proper serving of deception:

1. The absence of conscience. *You must be willing and able to betray and misrepresent anyone and everyone. If you are asked to sacrifice your first born child, do not hesitate.*

2. The ability to obscure your intentions and be difficult to read. *When you speak use evasive and general terms. Your face and movements must never betray your thoughts or feelings. Your eyes must remain speechless and you must rid yourself of that ridiculous nervous grin.*

3. The capacity to wordsmith and deflect. *You must always hide contradictions, doubt, and error behind strong words and dazzling speech. Moreover, to protect and/or advance your interests, in some instances you will be required to make weaker arguments—even if they are unmistakably wrong—appear to be stronger arguments. This skill is only honed through practice.*

4. The willingness to systematically annihilate anyone who is free-thinking and questions established or instantly conjured ideas, policies, and procedures that benefit the controlling majority.

5. Unfailing alertness. *The game will change, and no one will be eager to share the new rules or teach you how to play.*

6. Forged civility. *Pretend to like and value everyone.*

7. The capacity to make difficult and even erroneous choices. *Illogical decisions must appear logical to both the foolish and the wise.*

8. Occasional allies. *A list of individuals is enclosed. But remember, all allegiances are fragile.*

9. Strong resolve. *Be like a woman in childbirth. Even if the bloody bastard splits her from north to south or she must give her life in exchange for the child's, that woman will persist to the very end.*

10. Charm. *Appeal to everyone even when you know that they feel nothing more than unadulterated disgust for you. More importantly, at gatherings—small and great—feign interest with an occasional, courteous nod.*

11. Patience. *Rome was not built in a day, and neither will your career. Think short term and long term; some things should simply be plundered, while others warrant rule.*

12. Consistency. *Do not conduct yourself like an irrational woman whose mind changes like the weather.*

13. Contingency plans. *People and circumstances are unpredictable; therefore, like the chameleon, you must be able to adapt, blend in, and survive.*

The ingredients are uncomplicated and must be measured out based on your strategic intent, the personalities, and politics involved, and the circumstances. The key is to trust no one and make sure that every day the people you encounter eat what you serve. If this is any consolation to you, you only have to engage in the practice of deception until you are professionally and fiscally untouchable. Judging from your letters, that might take several lifetimes.

If you are hell-bent on me reading your professional obituary, contact my administrative aide and she will draft it for you.

Sincerely,

Albert Scélérat
Chief Global Strategist
Global Spectrum Alliance Inc.

Letter 10

Dear Clueless,

I applaud your efforts to commit yourself to chari-table causes. Nevertheless, please do not be excessively pleased with yourself.

Volunteering with organizations where the people look like you is a reckless exercise in futility. In short, it will ruin you. If you do not labor alongside causes that are located in the inner cities, ghettos, and barrios, you might as well be laboring in the dark. You will bring no glory to yourself, and your efforts will surely be vilified.

Give generously to charitable organizations and research foundations, but put your face next to ones darker than yours. Break a sweat alongside backs bent by poverty and dirty callused hands crippled by denied hope. I have found that engaging in activities to assist emaciated and poorly clothed children with swollen bellies and flies swarming about their snot-drenched noses is always a plus.

-Mr. Scélérat was called away to an emergency meeting and will be leaving for Bangkok later this afternoon. Per his instruc-tions, I have enclosed a list of companywide preapproved racially diverse causes, charities, and organizations that he strongly recommends you contribute "your time, average talents, and *wealth to on a regular basis." The highlighted items on the list indicate representatives from local media networks are usually onsite requesting interviews and taking pictures. Mr. Scélérat encourages you to make yourself liberally available to them, but to avoid smiling if you have not visited your dentist to have your teeth whitened.*

Mr. Scélérat also instructed me to inform you that "the game is like copulating: to truly reap the benefits, you must lose yourself in it—all the way to the very end."

For future reference, the one thing that Mr. Scélérat hates more than bad news is when bad news is either intentionally kept from him or the delivery of it is delayed.

Congratulations on the birth of your second child! You and Amina must be overcome with joy.

Respectfully,

Rebecca Bodhi

Rebecca Bodhi
Executive Assistant to the Chief Global Strategist
Global Spectrum Alliance Inc.

Letter 11

Dear Clueless,

Your last letter read like an oversized two-year old throwing a futile, yet entertaining, tantrum. *"I refuse to suffer anymore indignities and will discontinue working on projects led by incapable people."* Those *incapable people* can help to make or break your career. How have you grown so reckless and egotistical?

I fully understand that being in the precarious position of an in-house Negro is unpleasant; nonetheless, you must learn to acquiesce more readily to the politics around you, even, if your claims are just. In truth, no one gives a damn. If you remain stubborn and unyielding in your minority opinions, rest assured you will be sent to Willie Lynch's plantation to be broken like an outhouse Negro. And, I will personally finance your passage and training; you do still like training?

From your current position, the only things that are expected of you are: occasional reconnaissance, broad political compliance, and deferential *"sensitivity"* to those who possess some level of seniority. Whether you like it or not, this *"sensitivity"* must be provisionally extended to personnel who are not only verifiably incompetent, but also suffer from named and unnamed infirmities that conveniently intensify with every turn in the weather. I can only conjecture that it provides for them an imperceptible license to be miserable, crass, and fraudulent, while continuing to collect monetary compensation for regularly assigned duties they choose not to complete.

It is well-known that historically, their mysterious and reoccurring conditions cause them to prey upon and, without conscience, manipulate capable others like yourself into doing their work for them. Additionally, they tend to assume credit for accomplishments that are not their own. While this might infuriate you to no end, there are valuable lessons to learn and tactical advantages to be gained. More importantly, there is immense danger in inadvertently calling attention to the ineptitude of individuals whose competence and physical vigor are in question. Managers wanting in strength of character and common sense will always side with and advocate for them. I believe it is to make amends for the long-term effects of their own brutal incompetence. My only advice to you is to suck it up, smile, and continue to turnout great work because *I* wouldn't want it any other way.

Lastly, I cannot afford for you to be eyed with indifference and labeled an agitator. Granted, every now and then being a bit controversial is beneficial, but you have brought great damnation on yourself by openly supporting a rabble-rouser and organizational blasphemer. You young people are incorrigible. You not only behave far too hastily, but also in the absence of prudence. It is as if you and that damn Gremlin take some level of perverse amusement in creating senseless chaos. The Romans should have nailed you and that bloody Gremlin of a Comptroller upside down on a cross instead.

Replace the Gremlin with one of the frenemies identified on the list sent to you in a previous correspondence. If completing this simple task is beyond your middling abilities, I strongly advise that you remain a cunning organizational waif to avoid becoming the scorned village idiot.

Keep your stick on the ice,

Albert Scélérat
Chief Global Strategist
Global Spectrum Alliance Inc.

Letter 12

Dear Clueless,

Rumor has it that you and Gwyneth Heiwa are now cozy allies. I don't recall ever including her name on any of the lists that I forwarded to you. Maybe it's because she is the spawn of Satan.

Like yours, Gwyneth's promotion was not based on merit. The specs for the position that she now so arrogantly occupies were written to ensure that she could be clandestinely placed. Gwyneth is the quintessential, arrogant, organizational harlot. She earned nothing but parades up and down the corridors like a peacock in full bloom. Someone attempted, but failed miserably, to convince me that her promotion was in accordance with affirmative-action policies. How can that be when that division of the company is littered with women who look and dress just as colorless and unpleasant as she does? *Please do not send me a five-page answer to that obviously rhetorical question.*

I can clearly see why you were so easily ensnared in her web. Like me, Gwyneth is a charmer. She knows how to skillfully work both ends right to the middle. During negotiations, she makes all parties believe that they got what they wanted, but in truth, she got what she wanted. Understand this, Gwyneth is no ally. In fact, she is the worst type of enemy. When the chips fall, her primary goal is to always be on the winning side. She possesses no loyalties and answers to no one, but pretends to serve all. Quite frankly, she reminds me of Switzerland: neutral, diplomatic, economically prosperous, and politically impenetrable—a god to herself. I don't know whether to respect or loathe Gwyneth for her blatant, hypocritical acumen.

But, everyone has his or her quiver of weaknesses. For the most part, Gwyneth is predictable. While she sells ice to unsuspecting Eskimos, she takes sand to the beach and micromanages a colony of ants. She stubbornly wears her corporate longevity like a shrewd bullet-proof cloak.

Your alliance with her is a grievous mistake. Observe her, cautiously and closely, but do not acquire any of her malevolent habits. She is despised and, like an ostrich with its ass in the air, refuses to recognize it. Both eyes are open, but she sees only through the one that colors the world in her favor. People within her division work in fear of the lies she might intricately weave to place their reputations and livelihoods in jeopardy.

And to think, I was actually once married to her; though, that was very long ago and when there was considerably less of her. I suspect that the brief intensity of my domestic and organizational tutelage had a profound and lasting impact on her. God I wish that treacherous covertly uncivil sow would retire. Stay clear of her until further notice.

Cheers,

Albert Scélérat
Chief Global Strategist
Global Spectrum Alliance Inc.

Letter 13

Dear Clueless,

When I advised you to create a reputation for yourself, I did not mean for you to cast yourself in the role of Good Samaritan or civil rights activist. Which role do you suppose is more likely to strike fear in the heart of a church mouse, or subdue a feral dog muzzled and chained securely to an oak tree?

Good Samaritans are intellectual vagabonds executing futile deeds based on polluted piety and an endless need to be praised for misplaced charitable efforts, while civil rights activists are starved piranhas and hirelings that sermonize *equality*, *justice*, and *freedom* for the allegedly disenfranchised—words neither party can pronounce, spell, or define without inviting tempered laughter.

Perhaps the organizational strabismus you are currently suffering from is partially my fault. You have penned well over a hundred letters, but given the probable folly of their contents, I have found it unnecessary to pen a reply or even read most of them. I have failed you. No, you are failing yourself. Let me see if I can properly help you better understand how things truly work.

Behind closed doors, the Good Samaritan and civil rights activist both cackle like hyenas at the misfortune of those they claim to serve. Instead of becoming real players of the game, both try to distract themselves with *good deeds* so they will not drown in the piss of their mediocre success and uselessness. They are motivated by what inspires the very best and worst of us—the need for control.

Think of your work environment like the antebellum South. There are few masters, but many slaves of varying shades and abilities, each of them to be methodically and unforgettably screwed. You must always remember that people at the bottom rung of any organization, including middle management, are not paid to think. They are paid enough to shit and wipe their ass with course tissue. They are given a modest living wage (or less) to serve us, the better of their kind. All subordinates and what they produce are owned by the company in perpetuity. Thus, they can be used and misused irrespective of their wishes. It is the natural order of things. A true civil rights activist should know that the only *power* to the people is the one leveraged against them by quicker and, regrettably I must admit, sometimes duller minds. A true Good Samaritan should know that no good deed goes unpunished.

Clueless, professional milieus are supposed to be politically charged and polarizing. If they were not, I would have retired decades ago. Encouraging *good deeds* or *advocating* for those who have been purposefully silenced, will never transform organizational culture. Your efforts are not only futile, but also wasteful. If anything, it merely provides the ruling class with more ways to control and manipulate the suspecting and unsuspecting. You of all people should know that organizational politics follows its own moral compass on all matters.

Do not become the lone voice for a *movement* that has no possibility of gaining momentum. Somehow, you must discover a way to regain and sustain your focus. Remember the goal: to construct a monopoly over players and spectators of the organizational game—one that will place you at the fore within and without this company.

Since I am your mentor, I must warn you. If you continue to go against the status quo, you will pay and pay dearly. You will not only be marginalized and isolated by your peers, but also rot in your current position like dead flesh in a sealed tomb.

Warmly,

Albert Scélérat
Chief Global Strategist
Global Spectrum Alliance Inc.

Letter 14

Dear Clueless,

Ever since they downsized, reorganized your division, and named you director, your letters have become few and far between. While I do not miss your endless, rambling confessionals, what little you do write is even more uninteresting and useless to me. Be that as it may, your steady execution of my advice seems to finally be paying off. I expected no less. According to my raven, you have managed to curry the favor of many, as well as inspire loyalty from comrades and charlatans alike. But do not shit where you eat. I should receive updates of your progress directly from you and not some bottom-feeding informant.

At this level of the organization, and subsequently the political game, you must steel your mind. You cannot behave like a woman inexplicably affected and unhinged in varying ways by her monthly visitor. Every decision you make must be absent of emotion and undeniably duplicitous. As you are probably aware, your first order of business should have been to rid yourself of every potential rival and self-appointed organizational *leader* in your division. They are easy to identify. Brownnosers possess an incontrovertible stench. They are the ones who have an opinion about everything, think they can walk on water, are incessant flatterers, and are far too eager to take initiative. They spend their days jockeying for the opportunity to have protective time with you while simultaneously plotting your demise. Purge your division of them. If you cannot, you will spend countless hours proactively managing them and the mischief they produce. Search the company for agreeable worker bees, seduce them, and then fill your division with the thunderous sound of their buzz and the sweet product of their endless labor.

I am aware that you continue to suffer needlessly with a conscience, but to extend the boundaries of your influence, you must become a powerful practitioner of the slime effect. This means you must continue playing up to your superiors, but shrewdly treat every subordinate with pure contempt. They are nothing more than stepladders and stepping stones. None of that bloody insufferable *"the quality of my work should speak for itself and move me forward in my career"* business. As a director, you should engage in as little work as possible. Leave the labor to your best and brightest project managers, coordinators, and assistants. If you remain on the front line filling your nails with dirt and ash, you will render yourself impotent. Moreover, you will make a proper idiot of yourself, and of me. Power attracts power and, poverty of any kind attracts poverty of all kinds.

Lastly, I received the overdue, but comprehensive notes you took during the Chicago meeting. They were almost as enlightening as your first-grade doodling. I assume the additional stick figure with the oversized head means that you and Amina will be adding another pup to your litter.

Thinking the best of you,

A. Scélérat

Albert Scélérat
Chief Global Strategist
Global Spectrum Alliance Inc.

Letter 15

Dear Clueless,

At what point in our relationship did you develop such a blatant disregard for my advice? I specifically instructed you to guard your reputation like a lion guards the females in his pride. What do you do instead? Have lunch with Gwyneth—alone. You might as well have mounted a goat—in public. Did she leech you? That blood thirsty charlatan. Life robbed her of both delicacy and tact, but her parasitical talents are unmatched.

Anyhow, before a liberal thrashing, my grandmother always used to tell me that those who failed to hear would feel. As you are now aware, there are bitter consequences for individuals who cavort with fools and go against the establishment. You and I both know that within this organization—where integrity means nothing and reputation is everything—your actions were simply treasonous. For the life of me, I cannot understand why you are so fixed on squandering what little talent and intelligence you do possess on engaging people like her. You are playing the game like a clumsy, overloaded beast of burden. I would ask you if you were a man or a mouse, but given the circumstances, we both know the unequivocal answer to that question.

I cannot stress enough how imperative it is for you to avoid being sullied through association. There are several people you must never meet with alone (a list of names are enclosed). If it gives them a strategic advantage, they will throw you and your grandfather (God rest his bloody soul) under the bus. Shortly thereafter, they will devise a way to add public insult to injury.

I can only conjecture, that you wrote because you want me to assist with damage control to help ensure that your sparkling reputation will glisten again like newly polished crystal. I am of the mind to permit you to sit in your shit—at least for a little while. Nonetheless, I believe I have a proper antidote for your folly. But you must do something for me in return. Ms. Bodhi will contact you directly and provide details. There are just some things that should never be memorialized in writing, while others should be bronzed to cover and wipe your ass.

For now, find some way to make that lifeless project Gwyneth so effortlessly dropped in your lap succeed. Also, put your eager mind to the task of setting things right with the people who matter by not behaving like a brainless walking contradiction. For example, instead of going to all-you-can-eat buffets with the likes of frugal Gwyneth, spend your time properly engaged in political drama and forged diplomacy—playing the game.

Open your eyes and widen your gaze. Everyone can be bought and sold. To get ahead, everyone attempts to advantageously position him or herself to buy and sell. I know them all too well. My ledger is full of deals struck and bargains made. We are all pushers.

Clueless, every now and then, I see a very faint glimmer of hope in you, but then you nonchalantly dash it against a wall by acting mental. If I am casting my pearls before a witless swine, you should tell me now.

Good wishes,

Albert Scélérat
Chief Global Strategist
Global Spectrum Alliance Inc.

Letter 16

Dear Clueless,

Your correspondence read like a note from a school-girl with an unrequited crush. *"You will never believe who I had the honor and privilege to sit next to at the Innovation Gala"*. Get over yourself. You idolize someone you do not know, and at present, remains unproven in this era. The vice president of innovative initiatives is a lumbering, lackadaisical jackass. Yes, he was great in his time, but that was thirty years ago. The company's horse and buggy days are far behind us.

Have you noticed that whenever *your* vice president—the bloody paragon of organizational virtue and innovation—makes a decision, he blushes like some silly little girl whose secret of no consequence has been discovered (perhaps you two were made for each other)? Each gaffe is a public spectacle. He can't even lie without betraying himself and everyone else. Maybe I should offer him my mentoring services.

It seems like everyone (except for you) knows that he will be the death of this company unless he is replaced with someone more capable—someone like yourself. If your lower jaw has dropped, please kindly close it. Like me, you must learn to see first what others can only see in due course because of limited foresight and zero hindsight.

I have great plans for you. You should not dwell on that little fiasco that occurred last month. Like the tide, it has receded and your downward trajectory has been forgotten. I believe that your future contributions to the company will considerably dwarf your momentary lapse in judgment. Nevertheless, we have a considerable amount of work ahead of us.

Dethroning someone who spent well over twenty years to become an ill-conceived fixture within this organization will be no easy feat. Quite frankly, sending you and your family to populate Mars would be far easier. But, it must be done. And while we strategically depose him, I will quietly groom and recreate you.

At this time, you must work on transcending your current reputation as the company advocate for the weak and marginalized. Like Saul the Apostle from Tarsus, you have got to learn to become all things to all people so that you might win. To win, you must not only understand a person's language, but also his or her worldview. Become multilingual.

Furthermore, cease your efforts to *"restore a sense of honor and integrity"* among leadership through the ongoing indoctrination of middle managers and their brown-nosing squires. Ethically, we are all bankrupt. If necessary, we will sacrifice talented people at the expense of achieving the company's mission just to preserve the game. We do not mourn our deficiencies and neither should you. More importantly, it will not serve you to declare war on the faction that you so wish to eagerly join.

In due time, you will learn and accept that because this organization promotes haphazardly and incestuously, simpletons and incompetence abound. Although you do not make my job unproblematic, I will do my best to ensure that you are not named among them.

You have been properly forewarned. Do not permit the passage of time to weaken your resolve or question my decisions.

Godspeed,

Albert Scélérat
Chief Global Strategist
Global Spectrum Alliance Inc.

Letter 17

Dear Clueless,

So, *"hard choices"* trouble you, and your incessant whimpering tires me. How long will your conscience struggle under the unmeasured weight of reality? You must take after the maternal side of your family. I am almost certain that your grandfather would have had none of this peevish, insolent nonsense. First and foremost, stop using these ridiculous quotes to support your deviant machinations. The person who said, *"It's not personal; it's just business,"* is a god-awful liar and no truth will ever be found in him. It *is* personal, and the lesson is painfully expensive for individuals who allow themselves to think otherwise. Secondly, irrespective of type, business is always about the bottom line. Moreover, within the thick of that bottom line, pawns must and will always be sacrificed.

To remain at the forefront, domestically and internationally, we do not have the luxury of agonizing over every damn job lost or person replaced or displaced as a result of a merger or acquisition. I possess no empathy for people who are compelled to surrender their homes to make room for a new strip mall or highway. What little empathy I do have is currently reserved for the impending passing of Churchill—my true and trusted bull mastiff. Unlike you, he plays the game like his master.

I am completely aware that your previous letter and the nine that followed shortly thereafter are in response to the Tucson incident. Sometimes a very bad choice is the best choice—the only. Therefore, what exactly can you stomach? If making the hard but necessary decisions is not your forte, simply reassign culpability. Your current vice president is an ideal candidate for the position of fall guy. Use his name and the names of a few others (a short list is enclosed) to avoid taking responsibility for choices that must be made despite the inevitable backlash.

At all costs, your hands must remain unsoiled and your demeanor unfailingly neutral. While delivering *their* bad news, remember to feign sympathy for the affected party or parties. But do not over-do it. You must appear genuine. Take the romanticized approach if you must: *"It's not you. It's me."* If tempering language aids your fragile soul, then use it. Ultimately, it matters very little how you word it. At the end of the day, we better be ahead.

From time to time, I forget that it isn't your daughter still being breast fed, but you. I have a mind to contact the university that permitted you to graduate and request that it revoke your degree and dismiss every faculty member in its School of Business.

The world is a remorseless place. Business and politics is the unapologetic heart at the center of it. Before you write me again sniveling like an asinine cur, try remembering that.

My best,

Albert Scélérat
Chief Global Strategist
Global Spectrum Alliance Inc.

Letter 18

Dear Clueless,

It has been sometime since I received any correspondence from you. I cannot truthfully say that I mourn the absence of your bewildering literary creations. I thoroughly enjoyed the momentary respite. However, a periodic and succinct communication is always welcome.

I suspect that you are somewhere recuperating, or rather licking your wounds, after your little tryst with Gwyneth. Lying low is a prudent and useful tactic. Obviously, you have mastered it, but far too well. I must warn you that hiding as if you are a craven member of some small Amish village under attack by outside influence is objectionable behavior. At this juncture in your career, strategic visibility is quite expedient. Laboring in darkness, regardless of the quality of your work or the goodness of your intentions, is ineffectual. Your work must be as visually stimulating and unforgettable as your wife's recent breast lift.

Now that your personal quiver is obviously full, focus some of that prolific drive on pragmatically carving out a sure place for yourself within this political wilderness. You managed to do what very few people have done—verifiably resurrect and make successful one of Gwyneth's dead projects.

Establishing yourself as a force to be reckoned with and someone truly promotion-worthy is more about well-timed hype than anything else. You could be a second-rate vocalist dug up from a shallow grave in someone's backward that sings like a crow after a meal of putrid road kill, but if the industry determines that you've got "it" (whatever the bloody hell *it* is), you are the next untried cash cow.

From my perspective, and apparently the perspective of a few well-positioned others, you've got *it*. Although *it* is still questionable, inadequate, and untested, *it* is sufficient to get you where I need you and *it* to be within the next year. Get it?

I strongly advise that you emerge from the hole you crawled in before I create a painfully unfortunate circumstance to force you out. But, we both know that that could have been a fluke. Right now, you are still far too common. You need to start proactively separating yourself from the flea-infested, self-absorbed, ass-kissing pack in a more meaningful and incontestable way. Charm is not enough and, inevitably, neutrality wears thin. I want you to deliberately work on something that is categorically outside of your abilities—becoming peerless.

Cordially,

A. Scélérat

Albert Scélérat
Chief Global Strategist
Global Spectrum Alliance Inc.

Letter 19

Dear Clueless,

I found your question about whether to believe information carried through the *"company grapevine"* to be a bit disconcerting. You of all people should know that there is always some truth latent in any rumor. Whether you are capable of deciphering it is contingent upon your ability to separate yourself emotionally from the perceived issue and its players. Deciding whether the slightest hint of truth is consequential or inconsequential, and what to do with it, is an entirely different matter. For example, it was rumored that you were being relentlessly courted by one of our competitors. Imagine my absence of surprise when I discovered that this rumor was in fact entirely fallacious. Someone is being aggressively sought after by our largest competitor. It is that Asian gentleman in IT. I was informed that while he is exceptionally proficient in his profession, his speech was oppressively halting. Rumor has it he could barely put two coherent syllables together, but he knew his way around computer networks like a practiced prostitute. No one is up in arms over his pending departure. His kind are a dime a dozen. There are even some dimes that remember their professional courtesies and learn to speak fluent English.

People like you and me, however, are becoming a rarity. Well, me more so than you. You and the bloody Gremlin have firmly established that you are energetic, industrious, and possess some modicum of comprehension of the game. Nevertheless, and without fail, the both of you are awkward in your dealings. You ignore some of the basic principles of cultural politics and then expect it to go unnoticed or, even worse, for people to defer to you. What ninth planet do you currently reside on, the one formerly known to mankind as Pluto? This must undoubtedly be the case.

It has been said, and I believe accurately so, that great minds think alike, but fools rarely differ. Apparently, the Gremlin has been the catalyst for the recessed gene of stupid that resides within you to occasionally manifest itself. I could have sworn I instructed you to create sizeable distance between you and him. No, that was the curvaceous wench who is now working in my office. I frequently observe and, without judgment, fully appreciate what so afflicted you.

At any rate, no good will ever come of your association with him. It is undeniable that our industry shamelessly rewards innovation and ambition that thickens our bottom-line and augments our bonuses, but suffering fools, especially two of them, is far too expensive. The Gremlin is the emblematic court gesture, and you are slowly, but surely, becoming his faithful side-kick. Furthermore, he is far too frugal. He governs the organization's finances like a forty-year-old woman in a chastity belt. Is he above temptation? *"We are in an age where high moral standards should be the norm and not the exception..."* my left ass cheek. Prickly arrogant bastard. He can save his pious bleating for those wretched, marathon church services. His people are always trying to prove something. Mark my words, affirmative action might have gotten him here, but it will not keep him here.

The both of you suffer severely from some 1960's ideal that cannot and will not survive in this culture. If it is ever rumored that you and the Gremlin ran away together to join a Tibetan monastery, the truth of it would be all too obvious. I would not be shocked and simply wonder why it had not happened sooner.

Best wishes for your future,

A. Scélérat

Albert Scélérat
Chief Global Strategist
Global Spectrum Alliance Inc.

Letter 20

Dear Clueless,

"Pretenders" are an interesting group of people. Like city rodents foraging for food, the company is shamefully infested with them. I do not fault you for expressing some level of disenchantment and borderline disgust for these individuals. They are the colossal abyss into which the company blindly throws its money. However, even they can be useful instruments of great import.

You wrote that you have been *"experiencing some difficulty rooting out pretenders before they are staffed on major projects"*. Discover them, but let them be. The run-of-the-mill company counterfeit is easily identifiable and harmless. They sit heavily at their desks staring aimlessly at nothing. But it is the practiced pretender that is far more dangerous. They are the individuals who, once elevated, do absolutely nothing, but always give the appearance that their days are driven by a demanding and hectic schedule. The sophisticated counterfeits prance around attempting to establish their importance, yet they are inadequately prepared for every meeting they uneasily stagger into. Their mouths are open, but they say nothing, and eventually their words betray them. How have they been able to survive and thrive in such a politically charged organizational environment? Every court needs a few fools.

In time, the public persona of a pretender slowly and painstakingly unravels. They know that they will never be elevated beyond their current position. Consequently, they keep up with the charade and collect their paycheck like a low-level crack dealer. Needless to say, to a certain degree and on certain tactical matters, their voice possesses some sway. Regrettably, like a damn howler monkey, they shamelessly make people cognizant of it.

Since your ongoing associations with a couple of questionable lowborn colleagues might jeopardize your possible promotion to vice president, you will eventually have to create alliances with a few pretenders to gain a greater strategic advantage (a list of strongly recommended individuals is enclosed). Do not associate too closely with them, but every now and then, over a meal and a few glasses of something strong that will facilitate the loosening of tongues—their tongues and not yours—determine where their allegiances lie. Study them, but do not court mischief. Encounters with pretenders are less forgiving. More importantly, I am less forgiving.

Regards,

Albert Scélérat
Chief Global Strategist
Global Spectrum Alliance Inc.

Letter 21

Dear Clueless,

"Go green?" You never cease to simultaneously amaze and annoy me. You can *"go green"* and remain green as long as it keeps the company well in the black.

I am no longer under the impression that formal education has ruined you; it is unmistakably the case. You needed a graduate degree like I need a fourth wife. *Ms. Bodhi mailed you and your wife an invitation. Please leave your battalion with a capable au pair.*

The goal has always been and still remains to appropriately groom you into one of the foremost leaders of this company and not some damn tree-hugging environmentalist. Instead of writing these confounded letters that read like you have been gelded under an African cypress, you should be using the education that I so amiably and generously impart to you to further our strategic initiatives.

Do you know how much people pay to obtain my counsel? They salivate like Rottweiler's with rabies simply to hear me utter two words. Like a king, I summon them at will and compel them to wait for me with bated breath.

Yet I elected to make room for you—to personally mentor and teach you.

I am very aware that the past few years have been wracked with disillusionment and grievous lessons. If my memory serves me correctly, and it does, I do recall that most of it resulted from your own doing and undoing. Nonetheless, if you still intend to be successful, you must tame these childish, idealistic worldviews that are bricked so firmly in your head. No one goes unmolested by organizational politics. She entices all—breaks all— young and old, talented and talentless. She is neither the doting, dutiful wife nor the pleasure-producing mistress. There is no comfort in the allure of her breasts, and all bend under the weight of her piercing gaze. Her goal is singular: divide and conquer, enslave and oppress, rape and pillage. And although the possibilities are truly endless, she ensures that in some way, ultimately everyone pays, everyone loses—something. Be that as it may, for now, like a chaste woman after her wedding night, you must learn to better manage your expectations and endure your disappointment in bitter silence.

We must now focus on the future—our future. As you are aware, the vice president (that you so naively and nauseatingly worshipped) quietly submitted his resignation and the Board publicly accepted it. The position will be internally filled and not with another hapless simpleton. While several names have been bantered about, I tirelessly labor to ensure that yours remain at the forefront. In thirty days, you *will* be the new vice president of innovative initiatives because *I* believe in you. No, I believe in *us*.

Truthfully,

Albert Scélérat
Chief Global Strategist
Global Spectrum Alliance Inc.